A LITTLE JAMIE BOOK

WHAT DAY IS IT?

¿QUÉ DÍA ES HOY?

THURSDAY
jueves
18

WEDNESDAY
miércoles
17

SATURDAY
sábado
20

Little Jamie Books	Los Libros "Little Jamie"
A Day in the Life	**Un día en la vida**
My Favorite Time of Day	**Mi hora preferida del día**
On My Way to School	**De camino a la escuela**
What Day Is It?	¿Qué día es hoy?
What Should I Wear Today?	**¿Qué ropa me pondré hoy?**

A Little Jamie Book is an imprint of Mitchell Lane Publishers.
Copyright © 2010 by Mitchell Lane Publishers. All rights reserved. No part of this book may be reproduced without written permission from the publisher. Printed and bound in the United States of America.

Library of Congress Cataloging-in-Publication Data

Kondrchek, Jamie.
  What day is it? / story by Jamie Kondrchek; illustrated by Joe Rasemas; translated by Eida de la Vega = ¿Qué día es hoy? / por Jamie Kondrchek; ilustrado por Joe Rasemas; Traducido por Eida de la Vega. — Bilingual ed.
     p. cm. — (A little Jamie book / Un libro "little Jamie")
  Summary: A rhyming story in English and Spanish that follows a preschooler through a long-anticipated, fun-filled week's vacation at the beach.
  ISBN 978-1-58415-838-7 (library bound)
  [1. Stories in rhyme. 2. Vacations — Fiction. 3. Beaches — Fiction. 4. Spanish language materials — Bilingual.] I. Rasemas, Joe, ill. II. Vega, Eida de la. III. Title. IV. Title: ¿Que día es hoy?
  PZ74.3.K663 2009
  [E] — dc22
                                                                        2009028196

Printing   1   2   3   4   5   6   7   8   9

WHAT DAY IS IT?

A Little Jamie Book
Un libro "Little Jamie"

STORY BY/POR
JAMIE KONDRCHEK

ILLUSTRATED BY/ILUSTRADO POR
JOE RASEMAS

TRANSLATED BY/TRADUCIDO POR
EIDA DE LA VEGA

¿QUÉ DÍA ES HOY?

Bilingual Edition English-Spanish
Edición bilingüe inglés-español

Mitchell Lane
PUBLISHERS
P.O. Box 196
Hockessin, Delaware 19707
Visit us on the web: www.mitchelllane.com
Comments? email us: mitchelllane@mitchelllane.com

Today when I awoke I saw the sun was shining bright.
Mom was making breakfast and we had to catch a flight.

Hoy, al despertarme, vi el sol, con fuerza, brillar.
Mamá hacía el desayuno, y en avión íbamos a volar.

4

GATE 12
PUERTA 12

5

I've been waiting twelve whole months—or one year—just for this day; Through summer, fall, winter, now spring—hooray! It's finally May!

6

I packed my bags on
Saturday, preparing for
my trip.
The weekend went so
slowly, I was sure that I
would flip!

8

Hice mis maletas el
  sábado, me preparé
  para el viaje.
¡El fin de semana pasó tan
  despacio! ¡Creí que me
  volvería loca!

9

SUNDAY domingo	MONDAY lunes	TUESDAY martes	WEDN miér
1	2	3	
8	9	10	
15	16	17	
22	23	24	
29	30	31	

I peek over at my calendar
to see the day today.
It's time for my
vacation—one week of
fun and play!

*Miré el calendario para
ver qué día es hoy.
Llegaron las vacaciones:
¡una semana de
diversión!*

10

MAY
mayo

...DAY es	THURSDAY jueves	FRIDAY viernes	SATURDAY sábado
4	5	6	7
11	12	13	14
18	19	20	
25	26	27	28

12

If yesterday was **Sunday** and
today's a brand-new day,
What day is it, what day is it?
Today is finally **Monday**.

*Si ayer fue domingo,
y hoy ya amaneció,
¿Qué día es hoy,
qué día es hoy?
¡El lunes llegó!*

AIRPORT
AEROPUERTO

13

We flew down to the beach,
    where the breeze is warm and fresh.
It takes us all day long; when we arrive I'm told to rest.

Volamos hasta la playa,
donde la brisa es tibia y fresca.
Demoramos todo el día,
y al llegar, tuve que descansar.

WONDER FROG

15

16

Tuesday is a day of fun—
I run into the ocean.
Up and down and through
  the waves,
Splash! I make a commotion.

El martes nos divertimos:
me meto corriendo
en el océano.
Salto entre las olas.
¡Plaf, plaf, plaf!
Alboroto muchísimo.

17

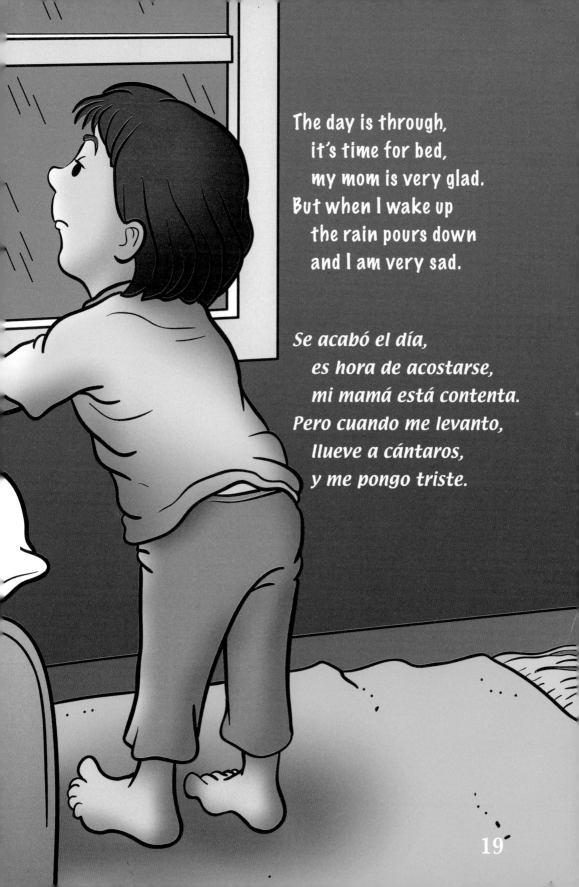

The day is through,
   it's time for bed,
   my mom is very glad.
But when I wake up
   the rain pours down
   and I am very sad.

Se acabó el día,
   es hora de acostarse,
   mi mamá está contenta.
Pero cuando me levanto,
   llueve a cántaros,
   y me pongo triste.

19

Is **Wednesday** a washout?
My mother tells me no.
To lunch and a movie and
shopping we go!

¿Perderemos el *miércoles*?
Mi mamá dice que no.
Nos vamos a almorzar,
al cine y de compras.

21

Wednesday flies by and
next thing I know,
Thursday is full of sun.
Outside to play, a walk in
the sand, and ice cream
for everyone.

El miércoles pasa volando,
y cuando me despierto,
el jueves está soleado.
Jugamos afuera, paseamos
por la arena, y hay
helados para todos.

22

24

A boat ride on **Friday**,
   we bump through
   the waves.
We see blue crabs and
   dolphins and giant
   sting rays.

Un paseo en bote el
   viernes, sobre las olas.
Vemos cangrejos azules,
   delfines y enormes
   mantarrayas.

25

26

On **Saturday**, our last day, I dive into the sea.
Bright fish and other creatures swim right under me.

El *sábado* es nuestro último día
y me sumerjo en el mar.
Peces brillantes y otras criaturas
nadan debajo de mí.

27

28

This morning Mom is packing. Vacation time is through.
I smile and think about the week:
    Each day held something new.

We're on a plane, back home we go.
    It's **Sunday** again, you see.
Next time for my week of fun, won't you please join me?

Esta mañana mamá está
    empacando. Se acabaron
    las vacaciones.
Sonrío y recuerdo la
    semana: todos los días
    hubo algo nuevo.

Regresamos a casa
    en el avión.
    Es domingo otra vez.
La próxima semana de
    diversión, ¿quieres
    acompañarme?

29

MONDAY
lunes

TUESDAY
martes

SUNDAY
domingo

TRASH NIGHT
sacar la basura

BALLET LESSONS
clases de ballet

PICNIC

Vacation may be over, but the days of the week
continue to bring new things to do.

*Las vacaciones han terminado, pero los días
de la semana continúan trayéndonos cosas
nuevas para hacer.*

30

THURSDAY
jueves

CIRCUS
circo

FRIDAY
viernes

MOVIE NIGHT
noche de cine

WEDNESDAY
miércoles

LIBRARY
biblioteca

SATURDAY
sábado

PIZZA NIGHT
noche de pizza

31

About the Author: Jamie Kondrchek earned her master's degree in elementary education from Wilmington University. She has taught pre-kindergarten and kindergarten. Jamie saw the need for read-aloud bilingual books that relate to curriculum standards for this age group. Since these books were often hard to come by, Jamie decided to develop her own collection, Little Jamie Books. She lives in Newark, Delaware.

About the Illustrator: Joe Rasemas is an artist and book designer whose illustrations have appeared in many books and publications for children. He attended Bennington College in Vermont and now lives near Philadelphia with his wife, Cynthia, and their son, Jeremy.

About the Translator: Eida de la Vega was born in Havana, Cuba, and now lives in New Jersey with her mother, her husband, and her two children. Eida has worked at Lectorum/Scholastic, and as editor of the magazine *Selecciones del Reader's Digest.*

JAMIE

JOE

EIDA

Acerca de la autora: Jamie Kondrchek tiene un máster en educación primaria de la Universidad de Wilmington. Ha dado clases de kindergarten y pre-kindergarten. Jamie se dio cuenta de que había necesidad de libros bilingües para leer en voz alta, que se correspondieran con los estándares del currículo para estas edades. Como estos libros eran difíciles de conseguir, Jamie decidió desarrollar su propia colección, Libros "Little Jamie". Jamie vive en Newark, Delaware.

Acerca del ilustrador: Joe Rasemas es un artista y diseñador de libros cuyas ilustraciones han aparecido en muchos libros y publicaciones para niños. Estudió en Bennington College, en Vermont, y ahora vive cerca de Filadelfia con su esposa, Cynthia, y su hijo, Jeremy.

Acerca de la traductora: Eida de la Vega nació en La Habana, Cuba, y ahora vive en Nueva Jersey con su madre, su esposo y sus dos hijos. Ha trabajado en Lectorum/Scholastic y, como editora, en la revista *Selecciones del Reader's Digest.*